AuthorHouse™
1663 Liberty Drive
Bloomington, IN 47403
www.authorhouse.com
Phone: 1 (800) 839-8640

Because of the dynamic nature of the Internet, any web addresses or links contained in this book may have changed since publication and may no longer be valid. The views expressed in this work are solely those of the author and do not necessarily reflect the views of the publisher, and the publisher hereby disclaims any responsibility for them.

Any people depicted in stock imagery provided by Getty Images are models, and such images are being used for illustrative purposes only.
Certain stock imagery © Getty Images.

This book is printed on acid-free paper.

ISBN: 978-1-7283-3083-9 (sc)
ISBN: 978-1-7283-3084-6 (hc)
ISBN: 978-1-7283-3082-2 (e)

Library of Congress Control Number: 2019920550

Print information available on the last page.

Published by AuthorHouse 12/21/2019

authorHOUSE®

Donny's mommy went into his bedroom to wake him up. He didn't ever sleep late. Donny was snuggled under his blankets. Mommy said, "Wake up, sleepyhead! It's getting late."

Donny wiped the sleepies out of his eyes and got up.

Mommy said, "Hurry up, buddy! Today is the last day of summer, and your friend Mason is coming over today to play. Tomorrow is your first day of kindergarten."

Last night, Donny had trouble falling asleep. He was thinking about kindergarten, and he was very nervous. He had crazy dreams about school. Donny wondered what his teacher would be like. Would she be mean like a *dragon*? Would he make any friends? What would he learn?

Donny sat at the kitchen table eating his breakfast. He was worried about school and he was very, very tired.

Mommy asked Donny, "Are you okay? Is something wrong?"

Donny knew he could tell Mommy anything. She always knew how to make him feel better.

He told her about his dreams about kindergarten and about his *dragon* teacher. He told her how scared he was.

Do you know what? Mommy said she was scared when she went to kindergarten too! Mommy said she even got nervous when she started her new job. Mommy told Donny that before she started her new job, she thought her boss might be a *dragon* too. That made Donny smile.

Mommy told Donny that she had a little surprise to give him after dinner. She said the surprise was going to make him feel a lot better about kindergarten. Mommy gave Donny a great big hug and kiss and told him that he was going to love kindergarten and his teacher, Miss Sandy. She also said that she knew for certain that Miss Sandy was not a *dragon*.

Donny spent the rest of the day playing with his friend Mason. They played hockey, they ate lunch, they played basketball, and they even had ice cream. Mason was starting kindergarten tomorrow too. Mason told Donny that he thought his teacher might be a *shark*. That made Donny laugh.

After dinner, Mommy went into Donny's room to give him his surprise. Donny was very, very excited! Inside the box were two things: a big, stuffed black-and-white dog and a tiny black-and-white dog key chain. Donny hugged the big dog, and he knew they were going to be great friends!

Mommy told Donny that the dog's name was Rocket and that he was a special dog. She said he was a School Pet who knew all about kindergarten. Mommy told Donny that when he fell asleep with Rocket, he would dream all good things about kindergarten. Donny thought that was so cool. Mommy also showed Donny the Rocket key chain. She said that she would hook it onto Donny's backpack, and then Little Rocket would always go to school with Donny.

Mommy tucked Donny and Rocket in, gave them both a kiss good night, and told Donny to have sweet kindergarten dreams. Donny hugged Rocket tightly, and they both went right to sleep.

While Donny was asleep, he had a dream about school again. Rocket and Donny went into his new kindergarten class. Miss Sandy was there, and she was *not* a dragon. She was a pretty teacher with a great big smile. The classroom looked fun. It had tables, chairs, crayons, games, and lots and lots of books!

Rocket showed Donny some of the things he would learn in math. He would learn how to count all the way up to one hundred. Miss Sandy would also teach Donny how to write his numbers up to twenty. Donny would learn about shapes and even how to add two numbers together. Donny was excited!

Next, Rocket showed Donny the reading area. Rocket knew that Miss Sandy liked to read all different kinds of books to her class. She even had a book about dragons! Donny loved when his mommy read to him, so he knew this would be one of his favorite activities.

Rocket told Donny that he would learn how to write his letters and even words. Rocket said Miss Sandy would teach Donny how to write his whole name.

Donny was excited to hear about the great things he was going to learn in kindergarten. He asked Rocket if he would also learn about dogs. Rocket told Donny that in kindergarten, he would learn about plants and animals and even the weather. Boy, was Donny excited!

Miss Sandy would teach the sounds of letters and how to spell words. Donny was working very hard on learning how to read with his mommy at home. Rocket said that Miss Sandy would help the students learn how to sound out letters and read words in kindergarten.

Rocket showed Donny the playground and told him that he would make new friends and even see some of his friends from preschool, like Mason. Donny thought the playground was really cool.

The next morning, when Mommy came in to wake Donny up for his first day of kindergarten, Donny and Rocket were snuggled up close together with big smiles on their faces. Donny opened his eyes and told his mom that he couldn't wait to start kindergarten. Donny got dressed for his first day of school, and then Mommy, Donny's sisters and Donny all ate breakfast together. Big Rocket even sat at the table with them!

When it was time to go to school, Mommy gave Donny his backpack and hooked his Little Rocket key chain onto it. She said that Little Rocket would always watch over him at school and that Little Rocket would be a friend that he would take to school every day. Mommy told Donny that if he got nervous or sad, he could just look at Little Rocket, and he would feel better.

Donny went to his first day of kindergarten, and he had a great day. He loved his new teacher, Miss Sandy— who was not a dragon—and he met lots of new friends. Miss Sandy read a book to the class, and Donny and Mason played on the playground with their new friends. Donny even made a quick visit to see Little Rocket on his backpack. Little Rocket gave him a quick wink!

Donny just loved kindergarten. It was so much fun to be with his friends and Miss Sandy and to learn all those new things. But most of all, Donny loved having Little Rocket there to share in his new adventure.

This is a picture of me and my Kindergarten teacher.

Your Name: _____

Kindergarten School: _____

Kindergarten Teacher: _____

School Year: _____

A note from my kindergarten teacher:

_____

_____

_____

_____

_____

_____

Joni DiCicco is an elementary school teacher in New Jersey. She has been teaching young children for many years and enjoys sharing stories and her love of books with her students. She enjoys working on curriculum development and student assessments. Joni has 3 children and lives in South Jersey. She enjoys spending her free time at the Jersey Shore.

Lightning Source UK Ltd.
Milton Keynes UK
UKHW022203050120
356245UK00010B/50/P